A Note About This Story

While researching my book *Stitchin' and Pullin',* a nonfiction account about the quilters of Gee's Bend (Random House, 2007), I visited Boykin, Alabama, about twenty miles from historic Selma. Mrs. Mary Lee Bendolph, a musician and a gifted quilter, graciously allowed me to stay in her home, where we spent hours talking about life in the rural South. When Miz Mary was growing up during the Great Depression, the all-black town was identified as the "poorest place in America." She told me stories about the many hardships she and her family had endured, and their struggle to survive in a segregated system that kept blacks locked in staggering poverty.

Yet when I asked Miz Mary how her family celebrated Christmas, the memory made her laugh out loud. "Before Santy Claus came to our house, Mama made us clean it from top to bottom," she said, her eyes sparkling. "We stripped away the old newspaper that lined the walls and kept out winter winds, and put up fresh new paper. One year, my sisters and I got a store-bought doll!" The excitement in her voice transported me back to that time and place, and I too experienced the happiness of opening that gift. It was from Miz Mary's brief recollection of her memorable Christmas doll that the idea for this book began to grow.

Jerry Pinkney's illustrations add another layer of interpretation to the telling, through bright images that seem animated—alive and vibrant. From the early scene where the family is repapering the walls with newspaper to the soft glow of that last picture, in which the children drink make-believe tea, Jerry has created a special family whose home, though poor, is filled with the richness of the holiday. We hope you wrap yourself up in the warmth of the season as you share this story of hope and love.

Happy reading,
Patricia C. McKissack

To Jordan Carwell—welcome to our family. —P.C.M.

To Pat McKissack, a bright square in literature's quilt. —J.P.

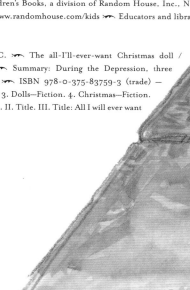

Library of Congress Cataloging-in-Publication Data ➤ McKissack, Patricia C. ➤ The all-I'll-ever-want Christmas doll / Patricia C. McKissack; illustrated by Jerry Pinkney. — 1st ed. ➤ p. cm. ➤ Summary: During the Depression, three young sisters get one baby doll for Christmas and must find a way to share. ➤ ISBN 978-0-375-83759-3 (trade) — ISBN 978-0-375-93759-0 (lib. bdg.) ➤ [1. Sharing—Fiction. 2. Sisters—Fiction. 3. Dolls—Fiction. 4. Christmas—Fiction. 5. Depressions—1929—Fiction. 6. African Americans—Fiction.] I. Pinkney, Jerry, ill. II. Title. III. Title: All I will ever want Christmas doll. ➤ PZ7.M478693All 2007 ➤ [E]—dc22 ➤ 2006030981

The text of this book is set in Mrs. Eaves.
The illustrations are rendered in pencil and watercolor on paper.
Book design by Rachael Cole

PRINTED IN CHINA

10 9 8 7 6 5 4 3 2 1

First Edition

the All-I'll-Ever-Want CHRISTMAS DOLL

Written by Patricia C. McKissack

Illustrated by Jerry Pinkney

schwartz & wade books · new york

Christmas always came to our house, but Santy Claus only showed up once in a while.

"Will Santy come this year?" my two sisters put me up to ask.

Mama tied on her apron. "One thing for sure, chickadees. He won't stop by if the house is dirty," she said, stripping the yellowed newspaper off the walls. Mama'd once explained that she called us chickadees because those little birds huddled together, chattering, twittering, and sharing everything they had—like us.

Filled with excitement, we began stuffing the cracks and tacking up fresh paper that would keep out winter winds, making our house ready for Santy Claus.

But I sure didn't want to throw away the page from the *Pittsburgh Courier* with the Baby Betty doll advertisement on it. Each night before falling asleep, I'd imagined us playing together.

"Baby Betty is all I want . . . ever," I announced the week before Christmas.

"Stop, Nella!" shouted Eddy Bernice, who never let me forget she was the oldest. "We're in a Depression! Why you wishin' for somethin' you ain' never gon' get?"

"Yeah, not in a million, zillion years," little Dessa added, giggling.

I flat-out refused to give up my dream. So, without my sisters knowing it, I wrote Santy Claus a letter and sent it all the way to the North Pole.

Finally it was Christmas Eve.

We all sang "Silent Night," and then we girls climbed into bed and snuggled under the new quilt Mama'd just finished. Daddy told us the story of a special baby born in a Bethlehem stable long ago. And even though we were too excited to fall asleep right away, the sandman overcame us one by one.

We were awake at dawn. "It's Christmas!" Eddy Bernice and Dessa shouted.

I leaped off the bed, bubbling over with excitement. "It's Christmas!"

Mama and Daddy stirred from behind their sleeping curtain. "What little mice-girls are disturbing folks 'fore day in the morning?" Daddy grumbled, pretend-acting angry.

"Merry Christmas, chickadees," Mama said, giving us each a sack filled with English walnuts, a peppermint candy stick, an orange, *and* a box of raisins. It was the most Christmas we'd ever had.

Daddy held one last package behind his back. "Merry Christmas, daughters," he said as he presented it to us.

There before us was a for-real, store-bought, brand-new Baby Betty doll, the color of chocolate, with rosy cheeks, black curly locks, and thick eyelashes. She was a million times prettier than I could have imagined.

"Ooooooo," cooed Eddy Bernice.

"Uh-hum," Dessa giggled.

"And she's mine!" I declared.

Dessa grabbed Baby Betty's leg.

Eddy Bernice elbowed in and snatched the doll's arm. "No, I'm the oldest!" she cried.

"Miiiiiiine!" Dessa wailed.

"Me!" I shouted.

"No!"

We tugged and yanked and shoved and pulled until Daddy separated us.

"Eddy Bernice Pearson, Laura Nell Pearson, Odessa Mae Pearson!" he said.

When Daddy called us by our whole names, in birth order, we knew we were in trouble. So we shut up and stood shoulder to shoulder.

Gathering us within the circle of his arms, he scolded, "Three times shame on you for fighting over a Christmas gift." He looked at us with disappointed eyes. "I have chores to do. Work this out and no more squabbling."

When the door closed, Mama turned to us and raised an eyebrow. "Okay, chickadees, fix it," she said. Then she walked away, holding on to *my* doll.

I spoke right up. "Who wanted Baby Betty the most?"

"You did," Dessa and Eddy Bernice answered grudgingly.

"And who said it was silly to dream about something I could never have in a million, zillion years?"

"We did."

"And who never gave up, and wrote a letter to Santy?"

"You did."

"So who do you think Baby Betty should belong to?"

Eddy Bernice shrugged. "You, I guess."

Little Dessa nodded.

When Mama heard we were all in agreement, she handed me Baby Betty, and the doll's eyelashes fluttered. "You are all I want. I don't need anything else!" I cried.

"We'll see," said Mama.

After I ate and dressed, I had the whole day to play with *my* new doll.

First I sang to her. *"You are my sunshine, my only sunshine. You make me happy when skies are gray. . . ."*

Eddy Bernice and Dessa watched for a minute, but when I didn't include them, they left.

Through the window I could hear them taking turns jumping rope with a measure of Mama's clothesline.

"Having you is more fun than any ol' jump rope,"
I whispered to Baby Betty. She blinked and I hugged
her tight.

I sang every Christmas carol I knew, from "Joy to the World" to "Jingle Bells." Baby Betty was a good listener, but my sisters always sang harmony with me, and Baby Betty couldn't sing a note.

"Oh, well," I said, rocking her gently. "Let's tell stories instead."

I began with "Goldilocks," followed by "Little Red Riding Hood."

When I finished, there was only silence. My sisters always clapped. But Baby Betty couldn't move her hands.

"Maybe you'd like 'Br'er Rabbit and the Tar Baby,'" I tried, and set in. At last I got to my favorite part. In my best storytelling voice I said, ". . . Br'er Rabbit say, 'Tar Baby, you'd better speak like you got some sense or I'll bop you upside yo' head.' But that Tar Baby didn't say nothing. It sat there in the road looking dumb."

That part always made Dessa giggle. But not Baby Betty.

I eased to the window to sneak one peek at my sisters. They were making string sculptures.

"I wish you could do something more than sit around like a spot on a toad," I whispered, a little disgusted-like. Baby Betty blinked.

"Having fun?" Mama asked, pouring herself a cup of tea.

"I guess so," I replied.

Then suddenly I got an idea. "A party!" I shouted. "Baby Betty and I will have a tea party same as Miz Florence, the lady you work for."

Quickly, I spread a quilt over Mama's trunk, then placed an imaginary cup and saucer in front of my doll. After serving, I took a sip with my pinky finger raised. "This is very, very delicious tea, isn't it, Miz Baby?" I said properly.

No answer.

I tried again. "I say, isn't this delicious tea?"

Baby Betty sat there. Could have been the Tar Baby herself.

"You'd better answer me, girl!" I shouted.

Nothing. Baby Betty was never going to utter a word.

"Okay," I said, throwing up my hands. "If you don't want to play with me, then I don't want to play with you either. So there." And I stormed away.

Through the window I could hear Dessa and Eddy Bernice chattering, twittering, and sharing. I felt like a lone chickadee.

As I stood listening to my sisters' hand-clap songs, Mama came over and put her arms around me. "I think they miss you," she said.

"Doesn't seem like it."

"Why don't you ask them to your party? I don't think Baby Betty will mind."

"You don't?"

Mama just smiled.

I didn't have to think about it long. I grabbed the doll and rushed outside.

"What do you want? We're busy," said Eddy Bernice.

I kicked at the ground. "Baby Betty wants you to come to our tea party," I said.

"She does?" Dessa asked.

"Mmm-hmmm," I said.

My sisters looked at each other.

"Who would get to pour the pretend tea first?" Eddy Bernice asked.

"You would," I answered reluctantly.

"And who'd get to sit at the head of the tea table?" Dessa put in, her arms folded across her chest.

"You would."

I hugged Baby Betty. "You know, she can't do much," I explained, "but she sure is pretty." Baby Betty's eyelashes fluttered and we all giggled.

Then I handed Baby Betty over.

All the rest of Christmas Day my sisters and I played with *our* doll. We sang Christmas carols in harmony and shared stories about *once upon a time*. Dessa knew just when to laugh and Eddy Bernice knew when to clap. We munched on peppermint candy and orange wedges, and ate one raisin at a time so they'd last.

But my favorite part was when I poured a pretend cup of tea. And with my baby finger crooked ever so daintily, I said real prim and proper-like, "Isn't this the best Christmas ever?"